GW00730491

Story ©2015 Katie Mullaly   Illustrations ©2015 Toby Allen
All rights reserved.

Published by Faceted Press, a division of Faceted Works, LLC.

No part of this publication may be reproduced, stored in a retrieval system,
or transmitted in any form or by any means, electronic, mechanical,
photocopying, recording, or otherwise, without written permission of the
publisher. For information regarding permission, write to Faceted Press,
Attn: Permissions Department, PO Box 682282, Park City, UT 84068.

Library of Congress Control Number: 2015908986

Land of AND / Story by Katie Mullaly / Illustrated by Toby Allen

ISBN: 978-0-9860997-1-7

Printed in the United States of America
First Edition November 2015
10 9 8 7 6 5 4 3 2 1
Typeset in Bembo Infant and Land of Type
The illustrations were rendered digitally in Adobe Photoshop®

Edited by Michael Rago
Book design by Faceted Press
The Yabbut™ and Land of... Children's Books™
are trademarks of Faceted Press

For information and resources visit
www.LandofChildrensBooks.com

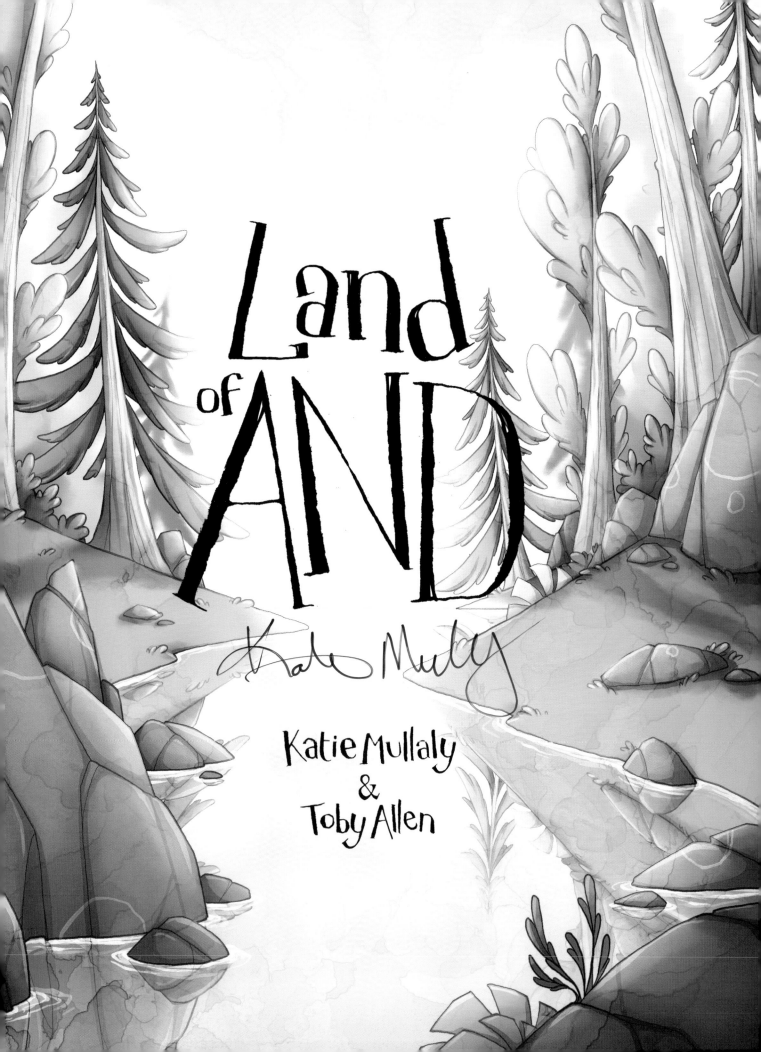

Land of AND

Katie Mullaly
&
Toby Allen

Well hello there, my dear!
Let me welcome you here,
To a river where everyone's going.

We'll become so aware
That there's much we can share,
AND include all we find as we're rowing.

To fill up our boat
Throughout our whole float
Will be an adventure so grand!

We'll embrace all we can
Floating down this long span
As we travel through Land of AND.

No, it's not just your chums
Invited to come
On our boat down this river to drift.

Bring the ones that seem strange,
AND it's you who might change
Because your opinions could shift.

Yes, our vessel is puny.
Adding more does seem loony.
But trust me, our boat is unique.

Our raft will expand
When you stretch out your hand
To ask them to float down this creek!

Come along for the ride!
Let me be your guide
As we journey on down this big river.

Let's put in our raft
AND launch this small craft
To find out what this trip can deliver.

First to join on the deck
Is one with a long neck,
And from other small boats it was barred.

Then the one with a snout
Who can sniff our route out.
It has skills we should highly regard.

You may not have thought
That these skills they have brought
Would be useful but now you can see

That unique's a great thing!
With so much they can bring,
They're in no way considered faulty.

Beware as we're gliding;
A creature is hiding
That's only around to bestow

Excuses for those
Who want to oppose
Allowing so many to go.

If you try to suggest
Bringing on all the rest,
It's the Yabbut that wants to refuse.

So please notice its tricks
To influence your picks,
AND include all we see on our cruise.

Now, behold that strange flock
Over there on the dock
With their feathers and colors galore.

A diverse bunch they are,
Some may think bizarre
'Cuz their style we've not seen here before.

Well, our boat needs more zazz!
Some razzamatazz!
AND this group will sure brighten our space.

Because we want to grab
Those uncommon and fab
AND not be afraid to embrace.

Now what can we do
As we float on through
With everyone that will appear?

They'll all want a job,
This excellent mob,
In helping us paddle and steer.

Let's give them an oar
AND make room for more,
So that everyone's **invite** is clear.

See the one in the shell?
It has stories to tell,
AND really just wants to be heard.

If it joins with our pack,
It can yammer and yack
Of adventures both wild and absurd.

There's so much to discover
AND learn from another.
New perceptions will be our reward.

So let's please not decide
To push it aside.
But instead we can bring it aboard.

But you don't want them all!
You say that one's too tall.
And besides, now you think they won't fit.

Very few to allow
Across the boat's bow?
Only similar we should permit?

And "Yeah but," you add,
"That one is plaid,
And I know it will surely annoy."

Well, that's no excuse
To exclude someone who's
Just distinct, and who we might enjoy!

You say you feel wary
'Cuz that one's so hairy,
And can't even see its own feet!

It has massive white teeth,
And it hides them beneath
Its fur until it needs to eat.

But it's nothing to dread.
Our fears we must shed,
Because it is really quite sweet.

See, different's not weird,
Or a thing to be feared.
It only means not just like you.

As we float through this land,
What you must understand
Is that you may seem strange to them too.

Look! There's one with more arms!
But don't sound the alarm.
It just wants to be **part** of our group.

Many oars it can clutch
To help paddle **AND** such.
What an **excellent** boost to our troop!

A peculiar outside
Can cause someone to hide
Because they were never **accepted**.

But since now we agree
They're just like you and me,
Let's take them to where we are headed.

Inclusion's a breeze!
You can do it with ease.
It's basic and quick, like a smile.

Or a "hi" just to cast
As we row on past
To all those we see every mile.

AND there's one that's dotted,
Who wants to be spotted
Hanging out on the river's far shore.

From now on we will greet
All of those that we meet,
And no longer choose to ignore.

Oh, there's one that's ready,
Who's stuck in the eddy
Just swirling around and around!

AND the one that's aloof,
But who's just a big goof
'Cuz it won't ever utter a sound.

They were constantly passed.
But they're picked up at last,
Since we chose to snag all that we found.

Were you ever passed by,
And you wondered why
You were left out and neglected?

They left you behind.
It was not very kind.
I'm sure you felt bad and rejected.

Oh, how glad you'd have been
If asked to join in!
Don't forget, please, how you were affected.

The rapids ahead,
How they fill me with dread!
'Cuz they're caused by the **Yabbut**, no doubt.

As we run this set,
The **Yabbut**, I bet,
Wants to make all the odd ones fall out!

But here in this land,
Inclusion's our stand.
AND everyone gets to stay on.

If we hang on real tight,
We will be alright
Until all of this whitewater's gone.

We are now at the end
Of our float, my sweet friend.
It was great to include and convene.

As our new pals now leave,
I'm so happy that we've
Shown them what acceptance can mean.

Each time you use AND,
Your world is less bland.
Remember this once you depart.

Just a simple hello
To the ones you don't know,
Oh, this can be such a great start!

Let them join in a game,
Or just ask them their name.
You'll help them feel like they're a part.

Inclusion can reach
Beyond just this beach,
And rub off on to those who now see,

That AND isn't scary.
In fact, it's quite very
A marvelous, fun way to be!

The End